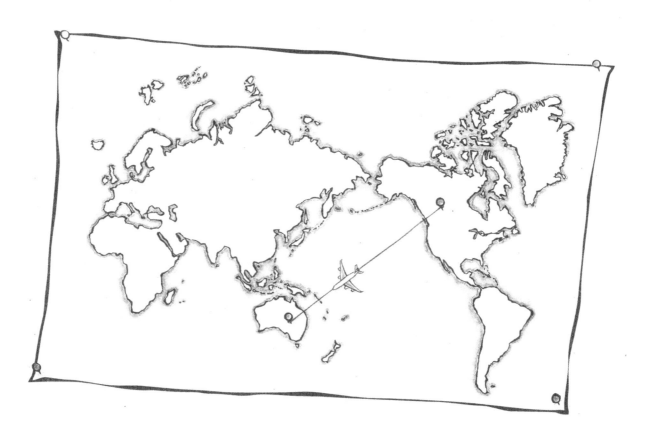

For Rob

Many thanks to Chrissy, Athena & Virginia

Published 2016 by Paper Bear
Melbourne VIC, Australia

ISBN 978-0-9944972-2-2

Text and Illustrations © Ardis Cheng 2016

This book has been typeset in Amatic SC and Cabinsketch

The right of Ardis Cheng to be identified as author and illustrator of this work has been asserted by her in accordance
with the Copyright, Designs, and Patent Act 1985.

Printed in Australia on 100% recycled paper

For more information about the author, visit: www.ardischeng.com

SIMONE

in Australia

Ardis Cheng

paper bear

Simone went to visit her friend, Jack, in Australia.

Jack lived in a big blue house near the beach.

When Simone arrived, it was very hot.

Simone had never been so hot in January before!

"Let's go to the beach to cool off," said Jack.

So Simone went inside to grab her things...

"It's as big as my head!" cried Simone.

"Oh that?" said Jack, "That's just a Huntsman spider. It's harmless."

And he swept it out the door as if it were a leaf.

Simone had never seen such a big spider before!

They started down the path to the beach.

Jack walked barefoot the whole way.

Simone had to put her shoes back on. The pebbles hurt her feet!

Simone had never walked barefoot outside before.

Further along, they passed a field full of...

The wallabies were
more Simone's size.

KAAA KAA

Simone heard a crazy laugh high
up in the trees.

"Whose crazy laugh is that?"
whispered Simone.

KOO AKA KAKKA!

KA KA!

"That's a kookaburra,"
said Jack.

"And that little spikey guy is an echidna," said Jack, pointing.

HELLO, MR. EE-KID-NA!

"And that tough guy over there is a wombat. They like to eat all the veggies in people's gardens!"

"What curious animals," thought Simone.

Simone had never heard of a kookaburra, echidna or wombat before!

Finally, they arrived.

"Welcome to Squeaky Beach!" said Jack.

SQUEAK!

Simone had never been on a
beach that squeaked before.

Squeak!

Squeak!

Squeak!

Squeak!

Squeak!

Squeak!

Squeak!

They went down to the water.

Jack dove straight into the waves.

Simone had never swum in the ocean before. She stepped in cautiously.

Oh, how the waves pushed and pulled!

"I think I've got the hang of it!" called Simone, when...

... down went Simone with a big wave!

She was used to swimming pools where the water stayed still.

SPLASH!

Jack and Simone towelled off on the beach.

Suddenly, a little creature popped out of the water! It was a...

... little fairy penguin!

One,   two,   three,

and many more.

They waddled across the beach and
into their homes in the tall grass.

Simone had never seen penguins away from ice and snow before!

"I've never seen ice and snow," said Jack.

"Never seen ice and snow?
Come visit me in Canada,"
said Simone.

I'll take you ice skating.

sledding,

and show you how to build a snow fort!"

"I've never been ice skating or sledding, and
I've never built a snow fort before!" cried Jack.

So they went back home to plan Jack's trip.

Quick Facts:

Huntsman spiders are the second largest spiders in the world. Their legs can be as long as 15cm (half a foot)!

Huntsman spiders help keep the pests away in the garden so if you find one in your house, it's best to catch it with an upside down bowl, slide a piece of paper underneath, carry it outside and set it free.

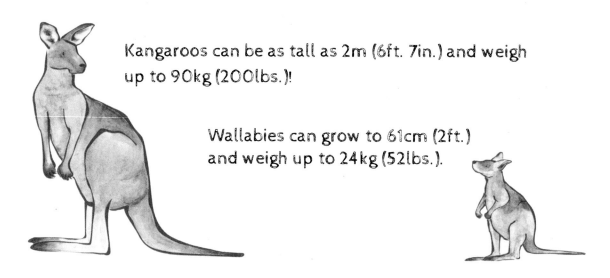

Kangaroos can be as tall as 2m (6ft. 7in.) and weigh up to 90kg (200lbs.)!

Wallabies can grow to 61cm (2ft.) and weigh up to 24kg (52lbs.).

Squeaky Beach is located in Wilson's Promontory National Park on the southeastern tip of Australia. The beach is composed of rounded quartz sand, which gives the beach its SQUEAK when you walk on it.

Little penguins (also commonly known as fairy, little blue, or blue penguins) are the smallest species of penguin. They are found on the southern coastlines of Australia and New Zealand.